MIDNIGHT CHRISTMAS WALTZ

Chronicles of the Westbrook Brides Prequel
A Sweet Regency Historical Romance

COLLETTE CAMERON

Blue Rose Romance®

Sweet-to-Spicy Timeless Romance®

MIDNIGHT CHRISTMAS WALTZ
Chronicles of the Westbrook Brides
A Sweet Regency Historical Romance
Copyright © 2022 Collette Cameron®
Cover Art: Angela Horner - Long Valley Designs LLC

For permission requests, write to the publisher at the address below.
Attn: Permissions Coordinator
Blue Rose Romance®
PO Box 167
Scappoose, Oregon 97203
www.collettecameron.com

eBook ISBN: 9781955259262
Print Book ISBN: 9781955259279

Dedication

For all families and their holiday gatherings.
"In family life, love is the oil that eases friction,
the cement that binds closer together, and
the music that brings harmony."

~Friedrich Nietzsche

Acknowledgements

To kick things off, I must acknowledge my cover artist, Angela Archer of Long Valley Designs LLC, for the breathtaking cover for MIDNIGHT CHRISTMAS WALTZ. She perfectly captured the essence of what I had envisioned to launch the Chronicles of the Westbrook Brides. Also, thank you to Cindy Jackson for expertly formatting and uploading my books to vendors, and to Dee for organizing the ARC team and promotion.

I'd be remiss if I didn't acknowledge the input from my VIP Reader Group, Collette's Cheris. Not only did you help select titles, but also hero names. I adore each of you!!

And last, but certainly not least, my fabulous editors, Christy Caughie of Gilded Heart Design and Beth Hale of Magnolia Author Services.

Thank you!

Introduction

Dear Reader,

I have spent over a year planning the Chronicles of the Westbrook Brides Series, and with this prequel novella, this long family saga is finally launched. I don't normally write an introduction to my historical romances, preferring to let you, the reader, dive straight into the story. But I've written this novella in a unique way—with several points of view to give you a peek into the characters' personalities whose stories you'll read first.

The Westbrooks are a large family (see the family tree at the end of the prequel), and I have no definitive number of books I'm going to write about them, though I have tentative plans for upward of twenty. (I have titles and characters for over twice that!)

You'll see foreshadowing in MIDNIGHT CHRISTMAS WALTZ, giving you hints about what to expect in upcoming stories. I've deliberately left several questions unanswered that will be fully explained in the appropriate lead character's romance.

I hope this introduction to a fiercely loyal, passionate, and adventurous family this holiday season fills you with warmth and joy as you begin this series chock-full of humor and intrigue. The heroes are charming, daring, and often scandalous rogues who would die for the spirited and unconventional women who become the Westbrook Brides.

Thank you for reading my books. I'm humbled and honored.

Hugs,

Collette

Prologue

GRANDMAMA

Hefferwickshire House rose garden
Duke of Latham's country estate
Late June 1825
Six months until Christmas

'*T*is completely unacceptable, Portia, and I shan't pretend otherwise.

Between them, Margaret and Haygarth have eight children. Eight!

And how many years has it been since this grand house saw a Christmastide with all their children present?

Or mine, for that matter?

Too many, I tell you.

In point of fact, there has never been a Christmastide with every one of my descendants beneath this roof. Not to mention, this Christmas also marks Garth's five and sixtieth birthday.

A celebration appropriate for the momentous occasion is in order.

I shall have to take matters into my own hands. I see no alternative. I'm too old to wait on the whims and peculiarities of capricious younger generations.

My health is not what it once was.

In truth, when Doctor Hartney, the younger, called upon me last week, he said my heart is weak, amongst other ailments that plague the aged. He also suggested bed rest and a reducing diet would benefit me greatly, the young quack.

Bed rest!

Me?

Never!

And what else does an old woman have besides her sweetmeats and her family?

I don't own a cat or dog to dote upon.

I'd dismiss him for his impertinence if he wasn't so

handsome and charming, and if I wasn't great friends with his father, now retired. Doctor Hartney, the elder, still brings me Turkish delights now and again. He did so just last week, though I was napping and Margaret accepted the delicacies on my behalf.

Nevertheless, my greatest desire is to see all my children, grandchildren, and great-grandchildren gathered for one Christmas, though I know it's immensely impractical.

Impossible, truth to tell.

However, I shall be satisfied if only Haygarth and Margaret's brood are here, singing carols, sipping mulled cider, stirring the plum pudding, and opening gifts.

If it's the last thing I do, my dear friend, Hefferwickshire House will overflow with Westbrooks, festivities, laughter, and revelry this Twelfth Night. I have a trick or two up my sleeve. My dear departed Roma grandmother, bless her, imparted a few gypsy ways to me when I was a child.

There will be miracles this Christmastide.

Naturally, you must come for a fortnight. You are

the sister I never had, and my family is yours. I shan't take no for an answer. You shall have the room next to mine, just as we did at school all those years ago.

Now to devise a plan and put it into action...

~Elizabeth (Libby) Westbrook, Dowager Duchess of Latham,

in a letter to her bosom friend of seventy years,

Lady Portia Borthwick-Pickleton, a childless widow

1

MARGARET

Six months later

Hefferwickshire House foyer

15 December — mid-morning

Ten days until Christmas

Humming *Joy to the World,* Margaret, Duchess of Latham, adjusted a holly sprig among the greenery she arranged in a Spode porcelain urn on the marble-topped rosewood half table in the mansion's entrance. Always her favorite time of year, this Christmas would be especially meaningful. Garth, her beloved husband, would celebrate his fifth and sixtieth birthday on Christmas Day.

Pausing in her humming, she tossed a wistful

glance toward the entrance where four footmen attired in festive crimson and gold livery filed past, their arms filled with cedar, holly, fir, laurel, bay, ivy, and mistletoe, while four more hauled in the yule log.

A pair of maids scurried behind them, sweeping up the inevitable mess bringing the outdoors indoors caused.

Eschewing tradition, Margaret had ordered the house festooned with greenery before Christmas Eve, and the decorations would not come down until after the last day of Twelfth Night. Something that brought such cheer and joy shouldn't be limited to just a few short days.

No indeed.

Margaret had even entertained the notion of decorating a tree as Queen Charlotte had, but such a special occasion ought to be shared by the entire family. Despite the festive holiday décor, her heart pinched behind her breastbone.

It had been so long since all of her children were here for the holiday, and in truth, she feared that day might never come again. Nonetheless, if it were just her,

Garth, Mother Westbrook, and perhaps, if their schedules allowed, Adolphus and Fletcher, then Margaret would make the holiday extra special for her husband of five and thirty years.

Their other children were either out of the country, had pressing obligations, or, as in the case of Darius and Layton, answered to His Majesty's Navy and Army, respectively.

"There you are, Margaret, dearest."

With a rhythmic *kerchunk, kerchunk* Mother Westbrook toddled into the foyer, gripping the carved ivory handle of her cane in her beringed right hand. The many bracelets at her wrists and pendants draped around her neck clinked melodiously with her uneven gait.

In another time and place, she might've been mistaken for a gypsy traveler.

A precocious twinkle lit her weak-tea brown eyes behind thick spectacles, and a hint of an impish smile hovered around the edges of her brightly rouged mouth.

What was the dear up to now?

One never knew with Elizabeth Westbrook, Dowager Duchess of Latham—Libby to her friends.

She'd never lost the spark of mischievousness that had first charmed Margaret when she, a widow with two young sons, had married the then formidable Duke of Latham, a widower himself.

"Ah, getting an early start with decorating." Mother Westbrook gave an approving nod as she took in the foyer, her keen gaze missing nothing. "Excellent. The house is never more glorious than when festooned with holiday greenery. I vow, 'tis an enchanted time of year. A time for miracles. One never knows what Christmas wishes might be granted, do they?"

Mother Westbrook also believed in fairies, leprechauns, wood sprites, Scottish brownies, and elves, or so she proclaimed. Margaret rather thought she simply enjoyed fairytales and make-believe. Or perhaps it was her Roma heritage that caused her inclination toward the mystical.

"Yes." Margaret also nodded, then stood back to examine her handiwork before glancing at her mother-in-law. "I want this year to be particularly special for Garth. It's difficult to share a birthday with the celebration of our Lord's birth. If all of our children cannot be here, well, then I'll make the season that much more memorable for him."

She might've married the duke out of convenience, but she'd grown to love him with an intensity that continued to amaze her. After all these years, shouldn't her love have faded? The romance have dimmed? How could it be that she adored the sometimes austere man so much that her heart was nigh onto bursting with love?

The Lord had truly blessed her when He brought Garth into her life, though at the time, she didn't recognize it for the gift it was.

If only their children could find similar happiness and contentment.

Layton, her eldest son by her first husband—a successful banker and merchant, but a vile human being—believed he had. That was until a decade ago, when Virginia, Layton's wife of two years, had run off with another army officer in the dead of winter. They'd both died in a tragic coaching accident, and he had since refused to entertain the idea of marrying again.

Wishing to raise the boys as his own, Garth had adopted Layton and Fletcher. He had done so in every way except for the ducal lineage. Primogeniture dictated that the title must pass to Garth's direct descendent and eldest biological son, Adolphus, the Marquess of Edenhaven.

"It shall be special. I just *know* it." The petite four-and-eighty-year-old declared with a sage nod of her silvery head and a thump of her cane for emphasis. Almost as if she knew something Margaret did not.

"The Christmas Eve ball shall be utterly magnificent." Mother Westbrook gave a raspy chuckle. "All of Twelfth Night shall be if we have our way. Yes?"

She cocked her head in the birdlike manner that Margaret had come to know meant her mother-in-law pondered something. Or she was kicking up a lark and plotting a bit of mischief.

"Yes, indeed," Margaret agreed, adding another holly sprig to the greenery. Tomorrow, she intended to make kissing boughs with the maids' help. Mother Westbrook's fingers had become too arthritic for the intricate task.

"I presume Cook has begun baking our favorite

treats?" Mother also possessed a sweet tooth, as her plump figure attested to. "Except for mince pie. Cannot stand the stuff. Whoever decided meat, spices, fruit, brandy, and sugar ought to be mashed together, plopped into a pastry, and baked must've imbibed far more spirits than the pie contains."

Giving a delicate shudder, she wrinkled her nose.

Where most elderly became sedate and mellow, Mother Westbrook grew all the more precocious and outrageous. Even her gown today, cardinal red and violet ruffles galore, eschewed acceptable fashion for a mature matron, as did the plethora of feathers poking from her coiffeur in no apparent order. Rather like pins stuffed into a pin cushion. Should a strong wind happen by, she might take flight.

"Mrs. Tastespotting has been busy baking for the past few days." Margaret collected her scissors before moving to another urn. "Gingerbread, fruitcake, marchpane, several kinds of biscuits, rum balls, and naturally, the Twelfth Night cake, as well as mulled wine and cider to start. Pies, of course, tarts, syllabub, lemon drops, and barley sugar candy…"

What else?

Margaret paused, searching her memory. "That's all I can recall off the top of my head. We'll have our usual Christmas goose with all of the trimmings, and this Sunday is stir-up Sunday for the plum pudding."

"Do make sure she prepares plenty. At least two puddings, I think." Mother adjusted a bow on her gown to her satisfaction, and the feathers in her hair bobbed in unison as the numerous bracelets tinkled at the movement. "One never knows who might pop in for a visit, and the Latham duchy is known far and wide for its generosity."

"I'm positive we shall have sufficient." Four or possibly five family members and the servants weren't a huge crowd to cook for.

"I do wish more of the family were gathering," Mother said, a trifle too offhandedly.

Enough for Margaret to cast her a suspicious glance, but Mother Westbrook—her eyes owlishly large behind her spectacles—blinked innocently.

Hmm. Margaret wasn't so easily fooled.

Mother had that meddlesome squint around her

eyes, and she shifted her gaze to the side.

Yes, she was definitely up to something.

The dowager fingered a holly leaf before sniffing a fir wreath adorned with gold, red, and white ribbons. Glancing over her shoulder, she asked, "No word from Darius or Cassius? Lucius? Leonidas? Or any of my other children?"

Did a mother ever stop missing her babes, yearning to be with them even when they became adults? For heaven's sake, Layton was eight and thirty, and Althelia, Margaret's youngest and the daughter she had despaired of ever having after birthing seven sons—two by her first husband—was two and twenty.

And in America. Where she'd been these past two and a half years visiting cousins after a heartbreaking episode had propelled her to flee England and seek respite with her aunt and uncle in Boston.

When Margaret recalled the incident, her blood still boiled, and uncharitable thoughts that would cause the devil to blush paraded through her brain. However, this was a season of forgiveness and joy, and she'd not let something that occurred in the past ruin the festivities.

Even if Ally would not be here again this year.

There was always next Christmas…

Margaret stifled a regret-filled sigh.

"Mother, you know Layton and Adolphus have not made amends. It's not likely they will ever voluntarily be under the same roof again."

An exchange of harsh words and even harsher fisticuffs five years ago had caused a rift between the adopted brothers that grew wider with each passing year.

"Nothing is impossible with the Lord, my dear." Mother regarded her unphased.

"Well, I'm afraid none of my other progeny has committed to joining us this year, and I've heard nothing from Garth's siblings either."

Pity filling her for her mother-in-law and a bit for herself, Margaret shook her head. "I cannot believe they don't care."

That was logic speaking.

Her heart felt something altogether different.

"Gathering for Christmas isn't as easy for them anymore," Margaret explained.

Or a priority either.

She could've bitten her tongue as disappointment and despondency flashed across her mother-in-law's crepey face. She had born six sons and had over thirty grandchildren besides the duke's offspring, whom she saw from time to time but never all at once.

A wistful smile curved the dowager's mouth as she shifted her cane to her other hand, also glittering with rings, and stared out the ornate windows on either side of the still-open grand double doors.

"Can you imagine, Margaret, how glorious it would be if all of my children, grandchildren, and great-grandchildren were here for Christmas? What a marvelous thing that would be, indeed. I should die a happy, contented woman."

"Hush. Don't speak of dying." After setting her scissors and ribbon aside, Margaret crossed to her mother-in-law. Embracing her, Margaret kissed her soft, lined cheek, inhaling the familiar rose and verbena perfume. "You still have many more years on this earth."

Mother managed a tremulous smile, wistfulness

creasing the corners of her eyes.

"The good Lord willing. Regardless, my Christmas wish is that the whole family would gather, if only for the ball."

That was as unlikely as Layton's sight being restored in his left eye or smooth, unpuckered flesh replacing the scars marring Lucius's face. Scars whose origin he'd never explained to the family.

Nevertheless, though her heart cracked the merest bit, Margaret fashioned a smile. "We shall have a jolly Christmastide, no matter who is present."

Or who is not.

"Of course, we shall." Garth strode into the entry, still a fine specimen of manhood, though his thinning charcoal hair had turned gray, and lines framed his indigo eyes and mouth. His dark green hunting jacket displayed still wide shoulders, and his Hessians emphasized long legs, muscled from daily horseback rides. "There's my lovely bride."

"Hardly a bride, my darling." Margaret's heart still fluttered when he entered a room. Silly goose. She put a hand to her hair and patted the carefully arranged curls to ensure none were out of place. "We've been married three and a half decades."

"And you are as beautiful as the day we wed." He swooped Margaret into his arms and planted a heated kiss upon her mouth.

Blushing, she slapped his forearm.

"Garth. Your mother is present."

"Flim flam and balderdash," Mother said, pointing her cane at Margaret and Garth, then wobbling it back and forth between them. "Family should show their love. All that prim and proper falderol about displaying affection in public." A naughty glint entered her light brown eyes. "Pshaw. I can tell you. Gerhardt and I caused a scandal or two in our day."

Yes, yes, they had.

Margaret recalled a particularly blush-worthy tale about a theater orchestra pit…

Encircling Margaret's waist, Garth pulled her to his side. "I quite agree. Husbands shouldn't care who sees them kissing their wives."

He dropped another peck on her nose.

Mother ambled to the door, her cane clunking on

the black and white Italian marble. She cast an impish glance over her shoulder and winked.

"Mark my words, you two. This Christmas will be unlike anything experienced beneath Hefferwickshire's roof before."

Premonition raised Margaret's nape hair.

"Mother, what have you been up to?" Before her mother-in-law could respond, gravel crunching beneath coach wheels filtered indoors.

A mud-splattered coach rumbled to a stop on the circular drive. Another laden with luggage lumbered down the drive.

"Were we expecting anyone today?" Garth asked, eyebrow quirked. "Someone for the holiday, perhaps?"

Did hope tinge his voice?

"No." Margaret shook her head, then gasped as the coach door sprang open and Althelia jumped down.

"Mama! Papa!" Royal blue velvet traveling skirt hiked to her calves, she bolted up the stairs, her face radiant with joy. "Are you surprised?"

"Flabbergasted," Margaret managed amid tears of joy, and then Althelia was in her arms.

"Uncle Reuban, Aunt Mary, and Mynna, Eva, Emerson, and Rogen came too!" Althelia said amid hugs from her father and grandmother. "All the way from America."

"I told you," Mother Westbrook said as Reuban, her youngest son, embraced her. "This Christmas shall be enchanted."

2

ALTHELIA

Hefferwickshire House dining room
16 December – morning
Nine days until Christmas

Stirring milk into her tea, as the Americans did, Althelia glanced around the breakfast table. She was home, and contentment and joy burbled behind her ribs. She tipped her mouth into a smile at the good-natured bantering between Papa and Uncle Reuban. She'd missed Hefferwickshire House, had missed Mama and Papa, her siblings, and Grandmama too.

And for certain, she'd missed Mrs. Tastespotting's scrumptious cooking. No one, absolutely no one, made scones as delicious and flaky as the cook.

Yet, Althelia couldn't regret her time away.

She'd fled England, a plump, awkward, and insecure mouse, and she'd returned slender, except where it counted most—and much more confident too. The splotches on her face had disappeared, her straight-as-a-pin hair had finally decided it wanted to be the same lush, silky auburn as Mama's, and, inconceivably, she'd grown another inch.

Althelia had discovered what she wanted from life; it wasn't the approval of the *ton* or young bucks. And certainly not that of vain, insipid chits who cared more about the ribbons on their gowns than people. Now she possessed the gumption and wherewithal to face those who'd humiliated her two and a half years ago with her head held high.

Just let them try to make a public fool of her again.

"So what are today's plans?" Althelia took a bite of coddled egg. "I don't believe there's a doorway, mantle, or banister left to decorate."

"And there are enough kissing boughs to assure no one escapes without a kiss or two." Her cousin Rogen quirked an eyebrow and jutted his chin toward the dining room entrance.

"I have no complaints about that." Papa winked at Mama.

Pink tinged her cheeks as she gave him one of their private smiles.

"What do you think about a venture to the woods this morning to find a Christmas tree?" Mama asked. "It's not traditional, per se…"

"Oh, let's do!" Mynna exclaimed, clapping her hands.

At eleven years old, the holiday still held a magical quality for her.

"I saw a Christmas tree once in Boston." Excitement lit her hydrangea-blue eyes and brought a flush to her plump cheeks. She clasped her hands to her chest. "It was the most marvelous of things ever. All lit up with small candles and adorned with sweetmeats, presents, toys, baubles, tinsel, and artificial snow made of cotton flocking."

"Like Queen Charlotte's?" Althelia spread a thin layer of strawberry preserves on a toast triangle. "A grand idea, Mama. Then we could spend the day making decorations. I'm particularly adept at paper cut-outs. Birds, snowflakes, stars, garlands, and the like."

Warming to the idea, she set her knife down. "Cook could make gingerbread men and other biscuits we can hang from the branches."

"I have plenty of ribbon left over too," Mama put in with a pleased glance around the table.

"And what will the men do while the women tend to those domestic tasks?" Althelia's cousin Emerson asked with a bored look from beneath his half-closed eyelids. "Go riding? Billiards? Perhaps a sojourn to the local village tavern?"

He perked up a jot at the latter.

Aunt Mary and Uncle Reuban sent dual frowns in his direction.

Putting her teacup down, Grandmama leveled him a censorial glance. "My boy, you will assist us. In fact, I think you shall be my personal bow maker. My fingers don't permit me the ability any longer."

She wiggled her rheumy fingers, the knuckles slightly swollen.

Althelia hid a grin behind the pretense of wiping

her mouth with a serviette.

Emerson was a good sort but cocksure and a bit full of himself.

"As you wish, Grandmama." He gave a stiff nod before taking a long swallow of black coffee.

"Perhaps we can go riding tomorrow?" After weeks at sea, Althelia longed to feel the wind brushing her cheeks as she rode hell-bent for leather across the meadows.

"*You…?*" Mama cleared her throat and exchanged an astonished look with Papa. "You ride now, dearest?"

"I'll say," Rogen put in. Just two years her senior, she and her cousin had become great friends. "Sidesaddle and astride, and she also sails a skiff quite handily. Oh, and Ally's a crack shot, not to mention nearly unbeatable at archery. Our Althelia has become a lady Corinthian."

Althelia chuckled at her immediate family's stunned expressions. "I told you I blossomed in America, thanks to Aunt Mary's and Uncle Reuban's nurturing."

"I'll say, my girl. And good for you. Knew you had

my gumption and temerity. Just had to find them." Winking, Grandmama cut a piece of ham. Fork in the air, she casually asked, "Been kissed yet?"

That sent Eva and Mynna into a fit of giggles. Emerson and Uncle Reuban chuckled while Rogen, infatuated with Althelia, glowered. A serene smile curving her mouth, Aunt Mary gazed on, calm and unaffected as always.

"Not for Gregory Bancroft's want of trying, the beef-witted bounder," Rogen muttered before stuffing half a sausage in his mouth and angrily chomping.

Aside from Grandmama's secret summons that Althelia must return home this Christmas—it was a life-or-death matter, which had still not been disclosed despite several delicate inquiries—Gregory had been the other impetus to leave Boston.

The man was determined to court Althelia, though she'd made it clear she was not interested in marriage just yet. She'd only come into her own the last year and a half. There was so much she wanted to do, places she longed to visit, and settling down to tend house and host gatherings wasn't at the top of her list.

Particularly in America.

Yes, she'd loved the two-and-a-half-year visit, but England was home.

Besides, Althelia rather fancied a tour of the continent. All she needed was a mature companion to accompany her. Or one of her brothers. Mayhap, Cassius. An artist studying abroad, he might be just the person. Or Leonidas, her world traveler, writer brother. But he hadn't been home in four years, and no one knew exactly where he was from month to month.

Oh, to have such freedom.

"I think the tree should go in the ballroom, so everyone attending the Christmas Eve ball can enjoy it," Mama said with a fond glance toward Papa. "And don't forget, it's also Garth's birthday on Christmas Day."

"I have a birthday gift." Althelia always made sure her father had both a birthday and Christmas gift from her.

"I require nothing more than a midnight Christmas waltz with my darling." He patted Mama's hand. "That's when I fell in love with her, you know, while the orchestra played *The First Noel*."

Tears stung Althelia's eyes, but she blinked them away.

Oh, to experience that kind of love someday.

Rambunctious laughter and pounding feet echoed in the corridor.

"What in the world?" Althelia glanced over her shoulder.

A commotion outside the dining room had everyone turning toward the entrance at once.

Arms thrown around one another's shoulders and wearing grins that split their faces, Adolphus and Lucius barreled into the room.

Simms, the butler, followed in their wake, a tolerant half-smile upon his face and happiness lighting his eyes.

"Happy Christmas." Adolphus bent into a silly courtier's bow. "One and all."

"Let the revelry begin." Lucius spread his arms wide. "*We* have arrived."

3

LUCIUS

Stir-Up Sunday

Hefferwickshire House's dining room

17 December

Eight days until Christmas

Just *how* many Westbrooks were expected for Christmas this year? As Lucius perused the room, he brushed his fingertips over the ridges marring the right side of his jaw from ear to lips.

Mama positively beamed as she spoke in low tones to Mrs. Tastespotting over the enormous plum pudding bowl.

Radiant herself, Althelia fiddled with the ingredients on the table.

By thunder, his sister had bloomed into a rare beauty. She'd shed her baby fat and become the intrepid young woman Lucius had always believed she could be. She just had to believe in herself. Perhaps having seven older brothers had been intimidating, but he couldn't be prouder of her.

Her gaze caught his and, grinning, she gave him a little finger wave and then blew him a cheeky kiss.

Lucius angled his head in response.

Agents of the Crown didn't flutter their fingers or blow kisses.

It wasn't dignified.

Arms folded and leaning against the fireplace mantel, his brothers forming a semi-circle around him, Papa looked on, a man content and still very much in love.

A twinge of envy speared Lucius.

This life—he swept his gaze over the revelers again—could not be his. Not in his line of work. A wife was a liability, a dangerous distraction he could ill afford. Furthermore, her life would be in constant peril.

And children?

Good God above.

No. It was unthinkable. Untenable.

His enemies wouldn't hesitate to use his family to get to him.

It had happened before.

There had been someone once—another agent. But she'd been killed, and the disfiguring scars Lucius now bore were an irrefutable testimony to the impossibility of him permitting himself to love again.

Grandmama approached, the top of her head barely reaching his shoulder.

Her familiar and comforting rose and verbena perfume tickled his nose as he leaned down and whispered into her ear.

"Grandmama, you've been up to shenanigans again."

He gave a pointed glance at the exuberant family gathered to stir the plum pudding and make a wish when it was their turn. There were so many aunts, uncles, and cousins here, the mixture would likely be watery goo by the time they finished.

Giving him a decidedly false, guileless upward sweep of her bright red mouth, she said, "Whatever are you referring to, dear boy?"

Unconventional, feisty, and full of spit and vinegar, his grandmother had made childhood a thing of wonder and adventure for her numerous grandchildren.

"*Life or death*? *Imperative I return home*? *Top secret*?" Winking, he nudged her shoulder. "Need I say more?"

"I had my reasons, which I shall reveal in good time." She patted his forearm. "Trust me."

That was the problem with Grandmama.

You couldn't trust the meddlesome dear.

Looking very much like the cat in the cream, she thumped her way toward Mama. The old girl was in her element, and who could begrudge her?

When was the last time she'd had this many of her children and grandchildren around her? Though she did walk a trifle slower than the last time Lucius had seen her, and she was somewhat paler. Frailer even. But wasn't that to be expected of a nearly five-and-eighty-year-old woman?

A burst of masculine laughter drew his attention to the far corner where Adolphus and several male cousins chortled over some joke or other. Adolphus raised his glass in a silent salute. The ducal heir was beloved by all, including Lucius.

Except for Layton, that was.

Though the idea was abhorrent, Lucius suspected Layton harbored hidden jealousy that he couldn't inherit the duchy. He might be wrong on that account, and so he'd never breathed a word of his reservations. Mayhap there were other reasons Layton and Adolphus had clashed in recent years. Why Layton had chosen a career in the army when he'd inherited a fortune from his father remained a mystery.

Dragging his attention back to the warm familial cacophony, Lucius drained his glass, then set it on the table. The brandy burned a fiery trail to his stomach.

At no time in his memory had there been this many Westbrooks under one roof. Mama had been compelled to hire several villagers to help over the extended holiday.

He was supposed to return to London no later than the thirty-first of December. Another dangerous mission awaited him. Arms folded, he leaned a hip against the dining table and stared at his boots.

His family only knew he worked for the Home Office, not that he was an agent of the Crown. A polite and benign definition for what he really was. A spy. A double agent, in truth.

He'd received Grandmama's urgent summons, as had Adolphus. And he'd wager so had everyone present in some form or other. He and Adolphus had compared nearly identical letters.

It is imperative that you return home for Christmas this year. I cannot
    divulge the details, but it is a matter of life and death. I shall not accept
    any excuse but that you are lying on your deathbed, about to cast off

your mortal coil yourself.

Lucius had been on a mission and only received the communication a fortnight ago when he'd returned. As luck would have it, he'd bumped into Adolphus at Brooks. Lucius had a leave of absence due him, so the brothers decided to humor their grandmother by putting in an appearance this Christmas.

Besides, neither had been to Hefferwickshire House in months.

A visit was long overdue.

"You'd best pray Layton isn't there. I haven't forgiven him, and planting our adopted older brother a facer wouldn't illicit warm holiday sentiments," Adolphus had said as they climbed into the coach two days ago.

Layton wasn't here, but that didn't mean he mightn't arrive later.

Surely, Grandmama had written him as well. She'd never distinguished between her adopted grandsons and those who were blood relations.

Lucius didn't know what had caused the quarrel between Layton and Adolphus, but he and Leonidas had broken up the brawling brothers and received a punch or two in the process for their efforts.

Lucius gave his empty brandy tumbler a wistful glance. He limited himself to one glass of spirits. A man in his profession needed his wits about him at all times.

Even at family gatherings.

Lord, he'd never seen this much of his family in one place, he mused again.

Not only had Uncle Reuban and Aunt Mary journeyed from America with four of their six offspring, three more of Papa's brothers, Edwin, Prentis, and Maynard, had arrived last evening with their wives and a slew of first and second cousins, most of whose names escaped Lucius.

He wasn't even sure which cousin went with each uncle.

No one could deny that the Westbrooks were a fruitful bunch.

Papa's two uncles had each sired four children, and

God only knew how many grandchildren. At least thirty between them. At least those branches of the family hadn't descended on Hefferwickshire House. *Yet.*

Then there were Papa's five younger brothers. Decent chaps all, and just as prolific as Father. Connell had fathered a mere five children, whereas Uncle Prentis, the lone vicar of the bunch, had sired eight. Edwin and Reuban boasted six progeny and Maynard had seven.

Lucius scratched his nose.

Odd that none of his siblings had wed yet.

Well, Layton had, but that tale didn't bear revisiting, and as he wasn't a biological Westbrook, the point was moot.

Would Lucius and his brothers and sister be as fertile as the rest of the Westbrooks?

From the laughter and chatter resounding in the room, he'd wager at least half of his cousins were present. And all were having a rousing good time too.

He smiled despite himself.

Such joy and merriment were contagious. Just as it

should be for a Christmas house party. Good thing Hefferwickshire House was a sprawling mansion that could easily accommodate one hundred guests. More if visitors doubled up and cots were brought in.

A sharp jab of regret stung his ribs.

He'd never have this.

Never be surrounded by his children and grandchildren.

Well, then Lucius would have the best, blasted, jolly good Christmas this year.

ADOLPHUS

Hefferwickshire House stables
18 December – late the next afternoon
Seven days until Christmas

Brushing the gelding's gleaming buff coat, Adolphus grinned at Althelia. "You've become quite the horsewoman, little sister."

"I've learned that with the right attitude and practice, I can accomplish a great many things." She patted the withers of the mare she'd just ridden. "Did you know I can fence now?"

She grabbed a small shovel used for mucking out the stalls and struck a pose. "*En garde.*"

"Never say that is my darling baby sister behaving

as a hoyden."

"Leonidas," she shrieked, dropping the shovel on Adolphus's foot and launching herself at their sun-browned, travel-worn brother. "I'm so happy to see you!"

"Ouch," Adolphus grunted before putting down the curry comb, toeing the shovel aside, and also embracing Leonidas.

By Zeus, after four long years, it was splendid to see his world-traveler brother.

How he longed for the freedom his brothers took for granted—envied their ability to choose their careers. His had been decided upon birth. Most men coveted his title, but a marquisate and future duchy imposed heavy burdens upon the recipient, including duties, responsibilities, and frequent complications.

He skewed an eyebrow skyward and twisted his mouth into a wry grin. "I presume you also received a frantic summons from Grandmama? Life and death? Urgent? Must come or the sun will fall from the sky?"

With a nod and a grin, Leonidas removed a satchel from behind his horse before handing the reins to Tobie, the stable hand. "His name is Orion, lad. Take good care of him, please. Extra oats. He's had a long journey."

"Aye, sir." Tobie smoothed a calloused hand down Orion's neck as he led the tired horse to a stall. "I'll treat him like a king."

Leonidas slapped Adolphus on the back, then wrapped an arm around Althelia's shoulders. "Indeed, I received a command to present myself, posthaste. If I hadn't spent a full two months in Rome touring and writing about the nearby ancient sites, the letter wouldn't have caught up with me."

Althelia puzzled her brow.

"No luggage, Leonidas? You're not staying long?"

"Never fear, Ally." He chucked her chin as he had when she was a little girl. "I was in a hurry to get here and chose to ride rather than take a mail coach. My belongings should arrive in a day or two. I honestly don't know how long I'll be in England."

Pulling a face, she formed her mouth into a pretend moue and shook a finger at him. "You had better not plan on leaving for a good while. We have much catching up to do."

"I should warn you, brother, the house is teeming with Westbrooks," Adolphus said. "Aunts. Uncles. Cousins. All of Father's brothers, their wives, and most of their children are here." Chuckling, he shook his head. "Egads, it's a maelstrom. But unexpectedly nice if somewhat chaotic."

Uncle Connell and his brood had arrived late last night, much to Papa's and Grandmama's delight. That meant all of Papa's siblings were in attendance.

That itself was no small feat.

"Never say so." Leonidas's raven eyebrows shot skyward. "*All* of them?"

"All of them," Althelia confirmed. "Mama is a bit overwhelmed, and Mrs. Tastespotting is near to having an apoplexy. Thank goodness the larder is full."

"It's no wonder," Adolphus sympathized. "She couldn't have been prepared to feed this bunch. But several villagers have been hired to help until Twelfth Night is over."

"Simms and Mrs. Bottleknob, she's the housekeeper now, have been running frantically for days too." Althelia shoved a burnished tendril off her face that had come loose during their ride. "No one sent prior notice that they were coming either." She wrinkled her nose. "More of Grandmama's doing, I think."

Hitching a shoulder, Adolphus scratched his chin. "I don't know half the relatives. But they're a jovial, friendly bunch. There is a passel of children, and I haven't even attempted to figure out who they belong to."

It was refreshing to be treated normally and not deal with sycophanting toadies merely because Adolphus was a marquess and a future duke. It wasn't often he was surrounded by people he didn't suspect of having alternative motives.

Even more welcome was the absence of posturing, simpering husband-hunting misses and their eagle-eyed mamas determined to make a brilliant match for their daughters.

It had been a long while since Adolphus could relax and be himself.

"I cannot believe you are here," Althelia said, hugging Leonidas again. "Mother will be beside herself. Papa too, though he'll act all dignified and proper."

She lowered her voice in imitation of their father. "Good to see you, son. You look well. How does the writing go?"

They all broke into laughter.

"Exactly so," Adolphus agreed.

She'd perfectly captured Papa's taciturn speech.

"Do you suppose Grandmama sent letters to all of our siblings and her children?" Leonidas looked between Adolphus and Althelia.

"Probably." Althelia nodded.

"And what is this urgent matter that required us all to be here?" Leonidas asked, brushing dust off his slate-colored greatcoat.

"She hasn't divulged that," Adolphus said as they exited the stables. The sun hung low on the December horizon and distant clouds held a hint of pinkish-gray.

It would snow by Christmas or he wasn't the next Duke of Latham.

A thrill of anticipation sluiced through him. He adored a good snowfall. It blanketed the landscape in virginal purity, peace, and muted silence that soothed the soul.

"I wish I knew what Grandmama was up to but she is as tightlipped as a priest," Althelia said, falling into step with her brothers.

Leonidas chuckled and swept a hand through his mussed midnight hair before replacing his hat. "Knowing our eccentric grandmother, she'll let us know when she's good and ready, and not a second before."

"I shouldn't be the least surprised if Darius, Cassius, Fletcher…and *Layton*"—Adolphus could barely speak his adopted older brother's name without familiar ire tunneling through his veins—"aren't here by Christmas Day."

It wasn't his blasted fault Virginia had been an immoral strumpet and propositioned everything wearing pantaloons. It *was* his fault that he'd said as much to Layton. He regretted that indiscretion. It had been unfair, unnecessary, and rubbed salt into an already raw wound.

And truth be told, he owed Layton a long-overdue apology. Even if he had divulged that ugliness five years after Virginia's death, hoping it would shake Layton out of his doldrums.

For Mother's, Father's, and Grandmama's sake, Adolphus had already determined to treat Layton with civil coolness should they meet. Far easier said than done, but the Christmas season called for a temporary truce.

Leonidas eyed Althelia. "I see America did you wonders."

"It did." She gave Adolphus a sideways, calculating glance.

"You ought to travel a bit before you marry, Adolphus. It would do you a world of good. I could go with you." She slid her attention to Leonidas. "Or *you* could take me with you."

Conniving minx.

"And what makes you think I am eager to wed?" Adolphus asked her.

"Probably because you are three and thirty and our sire was married twice by your age." Leonidas leveled him a smug grin. "Thank God, I don't have that expectation hanging over my head."

"You have no idea," Adolphus said, unable to keep the bitterness from his voice.

Leonidas drew to a stop and placed a hand on Adolphus's shoulder. "In truth, I do not. I apologize for my insensitivity."

Althelia put an arm around Adolphus's waist and gave a squeeze.

Oddly, of all of his siblings, his sister was the most like him. He'd adored her from birth, proudly carrying her around. Darius and Cassius too.

He'd always believed he'd make a good father when the time came. And he'd like a houseful of children himself. But finding a woman he could spend the rest of his life with presented a problem. Hence his continued bachelor status.

He glanced down at Althelia's auburn head, her jaunty hat slightly askew.

What Adolphus needed was a woman with his sister's temperament and spirit.

"Think nothing of it," he said.

They moved forward again, in silence this time.

What was there to say?

Adolphus's fate had been sealed from the moment he'd entered this world three and thirty years ago.

A cow lowed in a nearby pasture and a brisk breeze that portended snow assailed Adolphus's cheeks. Hefferwickshire's windows glowed a welcoming golden invitation.

"I think we shall have snow within four and twenty hours." He pointed to the dusky horizon. "Those clouds portend snow, for certain."

"Snow," Leonidas murmured, slightly awed as he studied the dove-colored sky. "I haven't seen snow in over four years." He shifted his attention to the long drive. "If our other brothers are coming, they'd best get here soon or they may find the trek impossible."

"Can you imagine how wonderful this Christmas will be if all of us are here, *and* it snows? I was a little girl the last time that happened." Althelia gave an excited, girlish skip.

Adolphus glanced down at her.

Yes, a wife who embraced life with the exuberance his transformed sister did might make marriage tolerable after all. Mayhap it was time he started a subtle search for a marchioness.

5

LEONIDAS

Hefferwickshire House grounds

19 December

Six days until Christmas

Half-frozen and unused to the bitter cold but having a devilishly good time pelting his cousins, Leonidas crouched behind a hedgerow, an arsenal of snow-molded miniature cannonballs near his booted feet.

Adolphus's prediction about snow had come true.

After dinner last evening, snow began sifting from the sky, just in time to herald the arrival of Darius, his twin, Cassius, and their other adopted brother, Fletcher, within an hour of one another. By morning, snow shrouded Hefferwickshire and the surrounding landscape in a fairytale-like tableau.

It was almost enough to make one believe in Christmas magic. If one were prone to fanciful beliefs as Grandmama was.

While the older relatives enjoyed a roaring fire, toddies, impromptu charades, and musical entertainment in the drawing room and salon, the gaggle of screeching, laughing children, overseen by doting parents and fussing nurses sledded down the sloping, snow-covered greens, made snow angels, fashioned snowmen, or simply frolicked in the winter wonderland.

Hot chocolate, spiced cider, gingerbread, roasted chestnuts, and games awaited them in the nursery should they become too chilled. Substantially more potent warm beverages had been prepared for adults who abandoned the outdoor play in favor of thawed fingers, toes, and noses.

Leonidas, Althelia, their brothers, except Layton, who had yet to arrive—if he was going to at all—and several cousins engaged in a fierce snowball fight. It came as no surprise that Althelia had opted to join her brothers and male cousins rather than embroider, play the pianoforte, or do something equally vapid as discussing fashion with their female cousins.

That would not have been the case a few years ago.

Jaw set to prevent his teeth from chattering, Leonidas motioned with his fingers for Darius, Althelia, and Lucius to circle to the left, while Adolphus, Cassius, and Fletcher approached the folly from the right.

Unfamiliar with the grounds, and also likely eager to find shelter, their foolish cousins had taken refuge in the circular stone structure and became trapped.

Darius stuck a snowball down his twin's nape, earning him a hard but good-natured shove onto his backside.

"Rotten blighter," Cassius grumbled, but his grin belied any true offense as he picked snow from between his neck and scarf. "You know I'll get even."

Althelia giggled, and Leonidas chuckled into the scarf encircling the lower half of his face. This was great fun. Not something he'd like to suffer regularly; he did value his appendages after all.

By Zeus, he'd missed his boisterous family.

More than he'd realized in the four years he'd visited one extraordinary exotic place after another. In the past three years, he'd published four books about his travels. It seemed people enjoyed reading about his adventures from the comfort and safety of their homes. He had no intention of giving up his sojourns to foreign lands, but more frequent trips home were definitely in order.

A confirmed bachelor at eight and twenty, he'd never considered marriage.

What woman wanted to be constantly on the move anyhow? Not to mention the discomforts and dangers he endured pursuing his dream to see and experience fascinating sites from Amazonian jungles to Egyptian pyramids.

No, Leonidas embraced his lot in life and had no regrets or complaints.

Besides, given the fertileness of the Westbrooks, he did not doubt that at some point he'd have a crowd of nieces and nephews to spoil. And when he was a wrinkled old man, he could regale them with his exploits.

He possessed a wanderer's spirit, no doubt inherited from his two-times Roma great-grandmama, and he doubted he'd ever be able to settle in one place. Good thing he wasn't the ducal heir or the spare. Such a mundane life would bore him to tears.

The shiver juddering up his spine and across his shoulders wasn't from the cold.

The mere idea of putting down roots gave him the willies.

"On my signal," he whispered, creeping forward, an armful of snowballs nestled close to his chest.

Thwap.

A snowball landed squarely between Adolphus's shoulder blades.

What?

Thwack. Thwack. Thwack.

Three more followed in rapid succession, all targeting Adolphus.

Leonidas hunkered down.

Blast it to ribbons.

Had the cousins outsmarted them?

Leonidas glanced over his shoulder as did the

others.

A sinister gleam in his uncovered eye, Layton hurled several more snowballs at Adolphus's chest and face. Layton rather resembled a pirate with the black patch covering his bad eye and diabolical smile contorting his countenance.

Other than blocking the miniature white cannonballs from smacking him squarely in the face, Adolphus made no effort to defend himself or retaliate.

"That's enough, Layton." Fletcher jogged to his side and blocked the next missile intended for their brother.

Darius and Althelia helped brush the snow from Adolphus.

"Not well done of you, Layton," she chided, pulling her eyebrows together in displeasure.

A welt had already begun to form on Adolphus's cheek and another on his forehead where he'd been unable to deflect the frozen missiles.

"I'm satisfied." Layton tossed the remaining snowballs away and rubbed his gloveless, red hands together. "Besides, he well knows it's no more than he deserves."

"Not quite the homecoming we'd anticipated, Layton. But I'm glad you came." Leonidas extended his hand, and Layton shook it before pulling him in for a hug.

"I've waited five years to exact my revenge." Layton notched his chin toward Adolphus, standing several feet away, thunder in his tobacco-brown eyes. "*He* knows why, and that punishment was hardly justice."

Six pairs of eyes shifted between the glowering brothers. No doubt each sibling was as curious as Leonidas as to exactly what had transpired, but none would probe. If Layton had wanted them to know the details, he'd have revealed them.

"Enough." Althelia grabbed Adolphus's hand and dragged him toward Layton. "You two need to make amends."

"She's right," Cassius said. An artist, he'd always been the most sensitive and religious of the children. The opposite in almost every way, except in appearance, of his much more daring twin. "We've all suffered because of your ongoing feud. It's time to forgive and put the past behind you."

Leonidas touched Layton's arm. "This is the first time, likely the only time, we will all be together for Christmas." He pointed to the hillside where the children yet romped. "Those are our first and second cousins."

They weren't Layton's and Fletcher's by blood, but in every other aspect everyone assembled was family. The Westbrooks born after Mama and Papa's marriage had never thought of Layton or Fletcher as anything but brothers.

That would never change.

His expression inscrutable, Layton shifted his focus to where Leonidas directed.

Leonidas then gestured toward the house. "Inside are relatives I've never seen before. But they came because Grandmama asked them to. She orchestrated this, and it's nothing short of a miracle that she managed it."

In truth, it was decent of Fletcher and Layton to come, which proved all the more that they *were*

Westbrooks, and not just in name but in spirit too.

Mama rarely mentioned her first husband, but, from all accounts and more because of what wasn't said than what had been, Everett Ellison had been a rotter to his core.

"What is the dire circumstance that required us all to be here?" Layton asked, bringing his attention back to the siblings, now standing in a semi-circle around him.

Raising his eyebrows, Leonidas shrugged. "Honestly, we don't know yet. Grandmama is being very mysterious. I, for one, suspect there is no urgent matter. She simply wanted her family to gather for what might be her final Christmas with us."

Alarm creased Layton's rugged features. "Are you saying she's dying?"

"No, not a bit of it," Leonidas assured him. "She's merely elderly. Frailer than last time I saw her, but that is to be expected."

"Although…there are worrisome signs." Everyone trained their gazes upon Fletcher. He'd studied to be a doctor, but, for reasons no one knew, left the profession and opened a high-end, very successful gaming club.

"Fletcher?" Althelia chewed her lower lip. "Do you…?" She sucked in a deep breath. "Do you think she is ill? Is that why she summoned all of us?"

Small puffs formed as she spoke, a testament to the dropping temperature.

Eyes narrowed in contemplation, he scratched his temple. "I've no way of knowing without examining her, which I vow she'll refuse to permit me to do. Besides, I'm out of practice, and I may be wrong."

But what if he wasn't?

What if Grandmama *was* ill?

"We concede. We're freezing," Rogen called as he, Emerson, and several other miserably cold cousins emerged from the folly. "See you inside."

With a wave, he and the others trudged toward the house's welcoming warmth.

"We should get out of the cold too," Cassius, always practical to a fault, advised. "I vow, frostbite is already assailing my fingers and toes." He slapped his hands together, then pulled his scarf over his lobster-red nose. "But I don't believe any of us is moving an inch until you two reconcile."

"True." Leonidas crossed his arms, prepared to wait them out, God save him. "If we lose an appendage or two, or end up with lung fever, the blame can be laid solidly on you two mule-headed sods."

Holding up his gloved hands, Cassius made a grim face. "I wonder if I can paint holding a brush between my teeth?"

"Well, I certainly cannot play cards or toss dice with *my* teeth." Fletcher nudged Layton's shoulder with his. "What will become of my clubs? Give over, big brother. Let's enjoy this time together. Don't continue to hold a grudge."

"He owes me an apology." Flint in his gray eyes, Layton met Adolphus's gaze.

Cupping his nape, Adolphus heaved a sigh. Regret creasing his features, he pressed his mouth into a taught line. "I was wrong, Layton. I never should've said what I did. I ask for your forgiveness."

"What exactly did he say?" Darius, always the most precocious, asked.

So much for respecting privacy and not prying.

"Never mind," Layton and Adolphus said simultaneously.

A reluctant grin tipped Layton's mouth upward.

Adolphus answered with a lopsided grin of his own.

Both being older brothers, mayhap they were more alike than they wanted to admit.

"Praise God and hallelujah," Leonidas said, stamping his feet and hoping his quickly numbing toes weren't permanently damaged. Just how long did it take for frostbite to set in? It would be deuced hard to explore the world without toes.

"Can we go inside now?" he asked. "I'm bloody frozen. I think my blood has stopped flowing."

"You'd be dead," Fletcher said dryly.

"Fine. I forgive you." Layton gestured toward the red-nosed, shivering siblings. "Not for your sake, but for theirs."

Layton extended his hand, and Adolphus gripped it before pulling Layton in for a hug.

"Oh, I think I might cry. Except, I'm no longer a watering pot. So I shan't." Nonetheless, Althelia gave a watery sniff and dabbed at the corners of her eyes with her scarf.

"Might I suggest the talk of Grandmama possibly being ill stays between us?" With a sweep of his arm, Leonidas gestured to his siblings.

A chorus of yeses greeted his suggestion.

If Grandmama was ailing, Leonidas didn't want the holiday ruined for her by outing her secret.

"Was it just yesterday that I yearned for snow?" Shaking his head, he said, "I temporarily lost my mind. Give me the scorching Sahara sands." He sent his siblings a challenging grin. "Race you to the house."

Laughing as they had as children, they dashed to the house.

6

DARIUS

Hefferwickshire House ballroom
The only room in the house besides the kitchen
where flour might easily be cleaned up
20 December
Five days until Christmas

Darius forbade himself to laugh.

It would be the height of ungallant behavior. He was a lieutenant in His Majesty's Navy. The son of a duke. Born and bred a gentleman from birth. Gentlemen did not laugh at the wiggling backside of women far into their ninth decade.

He pointed his gaze ceilingward. When that didn't help, he closed his eyes and sent up a silent prayer.

Lord, help me.

Peeking his left eye open, he gritted his teeth as hilarity threatened to overtake him.

Despite his best efforts, a laugh burbled up the back of his throat. He coughed into his hand, earning him a mirth-filled glance from his twin. Who, by the looks of it, struggled just as valiantly not to laugh.

In truth, merriment lit the eyes of several of those nearest.

A few intrepid family members, including Fletcher, Lucius, and Althelia, continued to brush flour from their faces, hair, and clothing after their turn at finding the bullet.

Giving a triumphant yelp, Lady Portia Borthwick-Pickleton raised her flour-covered face, a bullet clamped between her gums.

Lord, there was an image Darius would not soon forget.

Probably worse for his artistic brother, who drew and painted from memory and who, with admirable speed, concealed his half-horrified, half-dumbfounded expression.

Those assembled to watch or participate in the game, Bullet Pudding, enthusiastically applauded the elderly dame's fortitude and persistence. It had taken her some time to seize the bullet, but Grandmama's dearest friend from girlhood had persevered, despite having removed her false teeth.

After they'd fallen into the flour with her first effort.

Tall, reed thin, and attired entirely in black, Lady Borthwick-Pickleton was the opposite of Grandmama in every way. Since her arrival yesterday, she'd been like a child, eagerly engaging in one activity after another. As if she'd never had the opportunity before and fully intended to enjoy every second of the festivities.

Brava for her.

After a surreptitious inspection of the remaining flour in the large bowl, Mama clapped her hands. "Let's move on to Snapdragon, shall we?"

Yes, please.

Another table had been set up across the ballroom with the bowl of brandy and raisins. Family members swarmed toward the new game as Simms lit the brandy on fire.

A chorus of *oohs* and *aahs* went up at the impressive fiery display.

Cassius sidled up beside Darius. "Thank God. I was up next and truth to tell, Lady Borthwick-Pickleton's admirable endeavors left a great deal of spittle in the flour. I was going to plead a sick headache, even though Mama has mulled wine and tarts planned for after the parlor games."

Giving his twin a disbelieving look, Darius snorted. "You've never had a headache in your life."

"You know us artistic types. So sensitive." Putting the back of his hand to his forehead, Cassius struck a theatric pose.

His dramatic display earned him another contemptuous snort.

"You wouldn't be poking fun at my dearest friend in all of the world, would you?" Grandmama peered between the twins. An impish grin pleated her paler-than-usual face. Mayhap she'd applied rice power a bit too enthusiastically tonight.

After a furtive glance in her friend's direction, she

gave a conspiratorial wink. "I tell you. It was all I could do not to dissolve into a fit of laughter. Portia's face looked like a white goose's hind end. A *male* goose with *it* sticking out!"

Papa choked on the sip of champagne he'd just taken, and Leonidas, laughter dancing in his eyes, slapped his back. "Careful, Papa."

Leave it to Grandmama to say something completely inappropriate.

"I must go help the dear. Portia cannot see six inches in front of her face, and unlike me, she's too vain to wear spectacles." She toddled off, leaning heavily on her cane.

Darius still had no idea what the urgent matter was that had brought everyone together. He fervently hoped it wasn't what Fletcher had hinted at.

Having forgone his last four leaves, when Darius asked his commanding officer for time off five months ago, it had been granted without hesitation. The truth was, though this was his sixth year in the navy, he'd begun to rethink his career choice.

Would his parents, particularly Papa, be terribly

disappointed if he resigned his commission?

He loved the sea, always would, but he didn't particularly care for having no control over his life. Especially as he'd begun to consider marriage.

Oh, not now, but someday.

Sooner rather than later. He wanted a family, and he wanted to be a father. Something hard to do if he was sailing the seven seas, so to speak.

"I'm thinking about resigning my commission, Cassius."

Cassius gave him a considering look as he accepted a glass of champagne from a passing servant. "God gives us but one life to live, brother. If you're not happy in the navy, then by all means, move on."

He took a swallow and then glanced around at the merrymakers. "Any ideas what you'll do instead?"

"A couple. Nothing definitive."

A burst of laughter from those playing Snapdragon drew Darius's attention for a moment. Althelia held a raisin high before popping it into her mouth.

"Ally has had quite a transformation," Cassius said.

"She has." A proud older brother smile bent

Darius's mouth, "I'm happy for her."

"What has you two so serious?" Layton joined them, accompanied by Lucius and Uncle Edwin's eldest son, Torrian. "We're supposed to be gay and carefree, at least for a few days. Mama all but commanded it."

"Just discussing life and the choices we make." Darius stared pointedly at Lucius's scar, then Layton's patched eye. "And we all know neither of you lives a gay and carefree life."

"Darius is thinking about resigning his commission."

Darius shot Cassius a thanks-a-lot-you-traitor glance.

"Remind me not to confide in you again, Cassius."

"They understand your position better than anyone else." Cassius put an arm around his twin. "My art drives and fulfills me. But if I found something I was just as passionate about—I cannot imagine what that might be—I'd move heaven and earth for whatever that was."

Torrian, an unapologetic rogue, gave him a devilish wink and waggled his eyebrows. "I know what can do that, cuz. *A woman*."

An odd expression flitted across Cassius's face but was gone the next instant.

Darius nodded slowly.

He had much to think about until he returned to duty after Twelfth Night.

He'd give himself the next fortnight to make a decision and prayed he would make the right choice.

CASSIUS

21 December – late afternoon
Four days until Christmas
Drawing Room

Pencil in hand and sketchpad balanced on his crossed legs, Cassius whisked the lead across the page, sketching the cozy familial tableau before him. Cousin Eva played the pianoforte as the younger relatives gathered around the instrument and sang carols.

Grandmama and Lady Borthwick-Pickleton dozed in adjacent armchairs, while Mama and her sisters-in-law conversed in low tones, sipped tea, and attended to needlework. Papa and his brothers, and a few of the older cousins, relaxed in the adjoining room, smoking cigars and sipping a variety of spirits.

Althelia, her knees drawn up and head resting against the window sash, sat reading on one side of the window seat. Fletcher, long legs extended and crossed at the ankles, occupied the other half. Leonidas and Layton, expressions serious, studied the chessboard between them, and Darius had just beaten Adolphus handily at checkers.

Numerous other cousins played cards, wagering sugared almonds and other treats. Later, the children would come down and add a few more decorations to the magnificent Christmas tree in the ballroom.

All that was needed to complete the picture of domestic tranquility was a cat and dog. He paused, his attention shifting to Grandmama. Perhaps she wouldn't be as lonely if she had a pet to pamper.

He readily admitted he missed his family when abroad and kept up a regular correspondence with his parents and siblings, though Lucius, Layton, and Fletcher rarely reciprocated, and Leonidas's letters took months to reach him, so information was generally outdated once they did.

Of late, he'd considered returning to England, at least for part of the year. He'd completed his studies and needed to make a decision soon. More on point, the future he'd hoped to have with Constanza Segreti, the sloe-eyed, seductive daughter of the villa owner where he rented rooms, was marrying another. After she'd agreed to become Cassius's wife. It seemed that, though the son of a duke, he was neither rich nor influential enough to satisfy her ambitions.

He supposed he ought to be grateful he'd found out her true colors before they exchanged vows.

"You're very good. Excellent, in fact."

Cassius glanced up.

Approval and appreciation shone in Lucius's dark blue eyes, so like his own and inherited from their father.

"Thank you. I've had several portraits commissioned and made a tidy sum. I'll finish the last when I return to Venice. After that…?" he shrugged. "I haven't made up my mind yet."

Lucius propped his hip on the sofa's arm and swung

his booted calf back and forth. "Are you considering returning to England?"

After setting the pad and pencil on the rosewood and brace center table, Cassius leaned against the ruby brocade cushions and rubbed his nape. "I am."

"And...?" Lucius probed.

He'd always been like that.

Able to get information out of people, even if they didn't want to disclose it. Which was probably why he worked for the Home Office.

"Ideally, I'd like to establish a studio. Teach some, paint, of course, and continue taking commissions."

The problem was that cost a pretty penny, and while he wasn't a starving artist, he didn't have the funds to fulfill that dream. There was an off chance he could acquire a position at a school, but those generally paid poorly, and he'd not have the freedom to create as his spirit led him to.

Such were the conundrums of an artist.

Layton plopped down beside him, then picked up the sketch pad and proceeded to thumb through it. "Very impressive, Cassius."

Cassius tilted his head in appreciation.

"He wants to open a studio in England. Teach too." Lucius didn't even offer an apologetic smile for revealing the confidence. Hopefully, he didn't give over critical information as readily in his line of work.

Layton set the sketchpad down with a thoughtful nod. "You should."

Yes, Darius should.

He'd leave his heart in Italy if he did, but, in time, he supposed he'd heal.

The truth was, he'd been unable to paint since Constanza betrayed him, and Darius

very much feared that he might never be able to again.

Then what would he do?

8

FLETCHER

Hefferwickshire House library
22 December – nearly midnight
Three days until Christmas

Shoeless, legs extended, and his head resting against the sofa's back, Fletcher contentedly watched the crimson and orange flames playfully dancing in the fireplace through half-closed eyes. Warmth seeped into his bones, making him drowsy. Too comfortable to take himself off to bed, he took a long swallow of superior Scotch he'd helped himself to from the liquor cabinet.

As he had as a child, he'd sought out the library's peace and quiet. Reading helped to calm him and relieve stress. The multitude of Westbrook relatives teeming throughout the house was both wonderful and overwhelming.

Ironically, given his current occupation, he didn't like crowds but preferred to be alone or surrounded by a few intimate friends or immediate family. He hadn't minded the solitariness of practicing medicine, but other aspects…

Shifting and crossing one ankle over the other, he pointed his musings in a different direction. No regrets. He'd made a choice a decade ago.

The book he'd been reading, a rather awful gothic novel he'd hoped would take his mind off his current worries, lay face up on the gold and hunter-green striped cushion beside him.

He'd almost ignored Grandmama Westbrook's summons to appear for Christmas. After all, he'd only been to Hefferwickshire House thrice in the last ten years for the holiday. His businesses in London—a theater and two gaming halls—left him scant time for holidays. As it was, he couldn't stay through Twelfth Night but must return to Town the day after Christmas.

Someone was sabotaging his clubs. In truth, he

shouldn't have left London, but he trusted his second in command. If a crisis arose, word would be sent to him by special messenger and he would return with alacrity.

He'd sunk all of his inheritance from his biological father into the businesses, and although they were lucrative—very lucrative, in fact—the repeated vandalism, especially the fire three months ago, required costly repairs.

Besides, whatever the calamity was that his adopted grandmother had concocted to lure her extended family here seemed to have evaporated.

Likely, it had never existed.

Sighing, Fletcher drained his glass, then let it dangle from his fingertips.

The door creaked open, and he craned his neck to see who'd entered his retreat.

Althelia, wrapped in a thick woolen ivory nightrobe embroidered with blue roses, shut the door behind her before giving him a cheeky grin. Her auburn hair, so like their mother's, hung loose around her shoulders and brushed her waist.

"I thought I'd find you here, Fletcher."

One eyebrow shied high onto her forehead as she eyed the glass dangling from his fingertips. She sniffed and wrinkled her nose. "Are you pished?"

That brought an unexpected bark of laughter from him.

"Not even close, little sister."

He might operate a club, but he hadn't drunk to excess since the day he'd left medicine behind.

Without waiting for an invitation, she perched cross-legged on the sofa next to him. "I want to ask a favor of you."

Straightening, Fletcher set aside the glass and turned an inquisitive gaze upon her. "Why is it I suspect I'm not going to like what you propose?"

She fidgeted with the knot at her waist, then thrust her chin out. "I want to come back to London with you."

What?

He gaped.

That had not been what he'd expected, though, with this new Ally, Fletcher didn't know *what* to expect.

"I think not, Ally Cat."

"Don't call me that," she snapped, tossing her hair over her shoulder. Expression earnest, she leaned forward. "I want to learn about your business. Everything about it."

Eyebrow cocked, he tapped the sofa arm with his fingertips. "Why?"

"Because I plan on opening an establishment. After I travel for a few months with Leonidas. He doesn't know about that yet, however, and I'd appreciate you not telling him."

Fletcher couldn't help himself.

He burst into laughter.

"*Who* are you, and what have you done with my timid sister?"

"I'm serious, Fletcher."

He sobered and took her small hand in his. "I know you are, but my answer must be no. There are problems in London. I shouldn't even be here. It wouldn't be safe for you."

She screwed her nose up the way she always had when she disagreed. "Is it safe for you?"

No, it wasn't. In point of fact, he'd received two death threats.

But Althelia didn't need to know that. For certain she'd tell the others, and, before he knew it, Westbrooks would be swarming his establishments—although he had considered hiring Torrian Westbrook to investigate for him and still might.

Word had it Torrian was the best detective money could buy.

"I'll take your non-answer as a no, Fletcher."

Althelia unfolded her legs and scooted closer to him, laying her head on his shoulder. Peering into his eyes, she said, "Promise me you'll be careful."

"I promise." He patted her shoulder. "But enough talk about such a dark subject. Are you excited about the ball?" He tipped her chin upward. "Or are you worried something will occur like the last time?"

He hadn't been–there when she'd been publicly humiliated, but he'd heard about it. He wasn't the only Westbrook brother prepared to exact revenge, but Mama had reined in her angry sons.

Shaking her head, Althelia scratched her cheek. "I'm not worried. Mama has made sure none of the culprits or their families have been invited."

Good thing too, because not enough time had passed for Fletcher and his brothers to forgive the jackanapes and mean-spirited chits.

She raised her chin proudly.

"And I'm not the same shy, intimidated girl I once was." She gave him a vixen's grin. "Thanks to Rogen's tutelage, I now know how to defend myself and how to plant a facer. I can even shoot, and I'm dashed accurate too."

Skills she'd need if she were to ever own a club, but snow would blanket hell before Fletcher allowed that to happen.

"Come, minx. Let's to bed. I believe Mama has a full day of activities planned for us tomorrow."

She unfolded and rose gracefully. "I think she's overdoing it. She's been a bit peaked the past couple of days."

"No surprise. If I understand correctly, Grandmama

didn't give her notice that Hefferwickshire House was about to be deluged with family. Mama's probably not getting enough rest." Fletcher blew out the lamps, casting the library in dancing shadows. Once he'd adjusted the fireplace screen to make sure no sparks escaped, he cast a practiced gaze over the room.

A servant would be in later to double-check everything was in order and safe before retiring.

He and Althelia ascended the stairs in silence. Outside her bedchamber door, she hugged him. "I'm glad you came. I know it couldn't have been easy for you to get away."

"I'm glad I came too, kitten."

She despised being called Ally Cat, so he'd called her kitten from the time she was four.

"Goodnight, Fletcher. Sweet dreams."

She slipped into her room and closed the door with a soft snick.

"If only my dreams were sweet." Instead of the nightmares that haunted him.

With a sigh, he made his way to his bedchamber,

the same one he'd used since leaving the nursery. As he climbed into bed and relaxed against the crisp, lavender-scented pillows, he smiled.

It was good to be home and to temporarily put aside his cares. And to not have to constantly look over his shoulder.

9

LAYTON

Hefferwickshire House's upper-level corridor

23 December

Two days until Christmas

The pattering of small feet accompanied by excited giggles and whispers alerted Layton, and he stepped close to the wall as a troupe of shiny-faced children bounded around the corner, two harried nurses in their wake.

"We're on a thavenger hunt," a tow-headed chap of about six or seven and missing his front teeth announced.

"Scav-en-ger," a petite doll of a girl corrected, giving Layton a shy smile and trying valiantly not to stare at the patch covering his eye.

"Excuse us, sir." One nurse hurried to the front of the pack.

"Move along, children. If you want to win, you need to find a darning hook before the other children do." The other nurse, or perhaps she was a governess, spread her arms wide behind her charges, shooing them forward like a plump mother hen.

In the distance, more running footsteps and childish laughter threaded down corridors.

He'd bet his good boots the hunt was Grandmama's idea. She'd arranged many scavenger hunts when he'd been growing up.

"I have it on good authority that there is a sewing basket in that room. There might be a darning hook there." Layton pointed to Grandmama's solar, though if she'd ever darned a sock, he'd forgo Christmas pudding.

"Don't 'spose you know where t' find a cockle?" a solemn little chap with the Westbrook raven hair asked, giving the paper he held a dubious glance. "I dunno even know what a cockle is."

"Try the kitchen," Layton advised. "A cockle is a

mollusk similar to a scallop. It has a shell that closes."

He made an opening and closing motion with both hands.

"What happened to your eye?" This from the pretty little blonde doll.

A chubby fellow pulled his thumb from his mouth long enough to ask, "Are you a pirate?" before shoving the shriveled appendage between his lips again.

A hush descended in the corridor like January fog on the River Thames.

"My dears, we don't ask questions like that." The first nurse, her face a fiery patch of chagrin-induced blotches gave Layton an apologetic smile.

"Did it hurt?" the little girl asked, unphased by the rebuke.

He squatted, and the children gathered around him, their curiosity about the patch covering his eye momentarily taking priority over their fun.

"No, I'm not a pirate. Yes, it hurt." He pointed to the patch. "I lost the sight in this eye due to an explosion."

One that was meant to kill him so that his wife

could inherit his fortune.

The tiny blonde threw her arms around his neck and kissed his cheek. "There, that will make it all better. Mama says kisses heal boo-boos."

A lump of emotion wedged in Layton's throat, making it difficult to speak. He pressed two fingers to his face and cleared his throat. "Your mama is very wise."

"Thank you for your patience and kindness, Captain Westbrook." The governess smiled before taking charge once more.

No one had called him patient or kind in a very long time, simply because he hadn't been either. In fact, he'd been an assling to Adolphus. What his brother had said about Virginia, that she'd propositioned anything wearing pantaloons, had been crude, but not untrue. Layton's hell-fired pride had been beaten bloody to learn his wife had made illicit overtures to his brother.

After the nurses had herded the children into the solar, he went below.

Layton liked children.

Always had.

At one time, he'd hoped to have a houseful of sons and daughters too. That was before he'd vowed to never marry again. That sentiment had not changed, nor would it.

You could adopt.

The thought stalled him, one boot raised on the stairway.

By thunder, he could.

He had the means. He'd have to acquire a house, of course. And a nurse and governess.

Just how did one inquire about that sort of thing?

Lucius would know.

So would Torrian.

But he wanted to be discreet. Pride and all of that. He'd wait until the extended family had departed before poking around.

More lighthearted than he had been in a decade, Layton entered the drawing room. The rest of his siblings had already assembled. Next year when he came for Christmas, he might very well have a child or children of his own. And he'd make sure their Christmastide was as meaningful and magical as this one.

He checked a grin.

Look at him, already planning to be here next year. He'd have to thank his meddlesome step-grandmother. Had he not come to Hefferwickshire House for the holiday, Layton wouldn't have this new, optimistic outlook.

"You look exceptionally happy." Mama slid her hand into the crook of his arm. Weariness shadowed her eyes, but she wore a bright smile.

He grinned down at her. "I am. More so than I've been in a very long while."

"I'm glad. I worry about you." She glanced around the drawing room, her gaze resting on each of her children in turn. "A mother never stops fretting about her children. Praying for their wellbeing, provision, health, and happiness."

"You've been a wonderful mother, and you can be proud of your offspring." His heart full, Layton kissed the crown of her head.

Her eyes filled with tears, and she blinked rapidly.

"Save me a dance tomorrow, won't you?" She

pressed a palm to his cheek, below his damaged eye. "Who knows when we'll have the opportunity again."

He glanced over her head.

"I think Grandmama's manipulations have had the effect she envisioned. Every one of my siblings intends to make Christmas and Twelfth Night at Hefferwickshire House a tradition, and unless God himself stops us, we will be here. Every year from now on. You can count on it."

Epilogue

HAYGARTH

Hefferwickshire House ballroom

Christmas Eve

Five minutes to midnight

It was time.

Midnight was nearly upon them, and as Haygarth had that wondrous night so many Decembers ago, he bowed before his soulmate. "May I have this dance?"

It would be a waltz, of course.

Every year, he and Margaret enjoyed a midnight Christmas waltz. Perhaps when their children married, they'd share this Christmas tradition too.

Exquisite in a cranberry-red gown edged in silver lace with a delicate silver lace overskirt, Margaret smiled. The ruby and diamond tiara in her hair and the matching jewels dangling from her delicate ears and encircling her throat twinkled and glinted under hundreds of beeswax candles in the chandeliers.

He'd donned a crimson and silver waistcoat to complement her gown.

"It would be my pleasure." She placed her gloved hand in his and permitted him to lead her to the chalked dance floor.

After he bowed and she curtsied, they were in each other's arms, where they'd always been destined to be.

"I love you, Duchess."

Her pretty eyes softened and she stood on tip-toe to kiss his mouth in full view of their family and guests.

"And I love you."

A clock began to toll the midnight hour somewhere in the house.

"Happy birthday, my darling."

Garth glanced around the gaily decorated ballroom, taking in each of his children, the glorious Christmas tree, and lastly his mother, her eyes twinkling with a secret only she knew.

"It is the best birthday I shall ever have."

"How do you think Mother managed to get everyone here? I know she's behind this." He notched his chin upward in an indication of the festivities, children, family, and guests. "The children spoke of a crisis, a top-secret, and urgent matter, but I know of nothing that could incite the response she managed. Unless someone was dying, and even then, I'm not positive everyone would have arrived in time."

Margaret curved her mouth into an enigmatic smile. "You know as well as I do that Elizabeth Westbrook possesses ways, skills, whatever you wish to call it, that we do not understand. She brought us together because I think she simply tired of waiting for the children to come around on their own."

She arched her winged brows. "Don't be surprised if our children and her other unmarried grandchildren suddenly find themselves meeting their true loves. Given the size of our family, there will be a slew of Westbrook brides."

The music faded and the waltz ended, followed by polite applause.

Lips trembling as she surveyed the ballroom, a tear escaped the corner of Margaret's eye.

"Mama, whatever is wrong?" Althelia hurried to their mother's side and put a comforting arm around her shoulder.

"Nothing is wrong, my darling child." Face radiant, Margaret swiped a bent knuckle under each eye. "Everything is right and just as it should be. Our family is together once more."

"That calls for a toast." Garth signaled for Simms to oversee the pouring of champagne for everyone.

Their children gathered close with him, Margaret, and Mother at the center and the extended family and guests, including Lady Borthwick-Pickleton, on the perimeter.

Garth raised his glass. "To Family."

Everyone lifted their flutes and a chorus of "To Family" echoed around the ballroom.

"Happy Christmas to all," Grandmama said.

Yes, no matter where life took the Westbrooks, what triumphs or tragedies befell them, they would always have each other.

About the Author

USA Today Bestselling, award-winning author COLLETTE CAMERON® scribbles Scottish and Regency historicals featuring dashing rogues and scoundrels and the intrepid damsels who reform them. Blessed with an overactive and witty muse that won't stop whispering new romantic romps in her ear, she's lived in Oregon her entire life, though she dreams of living in Scotland part-time. A self-confessed Cadbury chocoholic, you'll always find a dash of inspiration and a pinch of humor in her sweet-to-spicy timeless romances®.

Explore **Collette's worlds** at
www.collettecameron.com!

Join her **VIP Reader Club** and **FREE newsletter**.
Giggles guaranteed!

FREE BOOK: Join Collette's The Regency Rose®
VIP Reader Club to get updates on book releases, cover
reveals, contests, and giveaways she reserves
exclusively for email and newsletter followers. Also,
any deals, sales, or special promotions are offered to
club members first. She will not share your name or
email, nor will she spam you.

http://bit.ly/TheRegencyRoseGift

Follow Collette on BookBub
www.bookbub.com/authors/collette-cameron

Other Collette Cameron Books

Chronicles of the Westbrook Brides

Midnight Christmas Waltz

Mission at Midnight – *Coming Soon*

The Midnight Marquess – *Coming Soon*

Minuet at Midnight – *Coming Soon*

Moonlight Wishes & Midnight Kisses – *Coming Soon*

Holly, Mistletoe, & Midnight Snow – *Coming Soon*

Wishing Upon a Midnight Star – *Coming Soon*

Kiss a Rake at Midnight – *Coming Soon*

Unmasked at Midnight – *Coming Soon*

Once Upon a Midnight Dream - *Coming Soon*

The Wallflower's Midnight Waltz – *Coming Soon*

Memories Made at Midnight – *Coming Soon*

Check out Collette's Other Series

Daughters of Desire

Highland Heather Romancing a Scot

The Culpepper Misses

Heart of a Scot

Castle Brides

Seductive Scoundrels

The Honorable Rogues®

Collections

Lords in Love

Heart of a Scot Books 1-3

The Honorable Rogues® Books 1-3

The Honorable Rogues® Books 4-6

Seductive Scoundrels Series Books 1-3

Seductive Scoundrels Series Books 4-6

The Culpepper Misses Series Books 1-2

~Coming Soon~

Daughters of Desire (Scandalous Ladies) Series Books 1-2

Highland Heather Romancing a Scot Series Books 1-2

Thank you for reading MIDNIGHT CHRISTMAS WALTZ, the prequel to the CHRONICLES OF THE WESTBROOK BRIDES. As I mentioned in the introduction, I took artistic liberty and wrote the story from the points of view of several of the characters you'll see in future books. I've deliberately left questions unanswered in the prequel that will be fully explained in each lead character's romance.

These stories are sweet, meaning they don't contain any graphic sex or foul language, though I do allow for sexual tension and realistic exclamations. Also, I didn't include a chapter for Cortland Marlow-Westbrook in this prequel. He was introduced in WHEN A DUKE DESIRES A LASS, Seductive Scoundrels Series, and his story is among the first in the Chronicles of the Westbrook Brides Series.

Though many attribute Prince Albert as the first to introduce the German tradition of Christmas trees to England, it was Queen Charlotte who did so in 1800 with a yew tree, rather than a fir. The decorations I described in this story have been credited to the yew bows and trees she oversaw the decorating of. Traditionally, houses weren't adorned with greenery until Christmas Eve, but I have no doubt families eschewed that tradition, as Margaret did, and decorated their homes before the official date.

I also mentioned Turkish delight in the story. It was introduced to England in the 19th century, but I was unable to find an exact date. Again, I took a bit of liberty and let Grandmama enjoy the confection early on. Who could begrudge the delightful lady her treat?

However, Grandmama is not a fan of mince pie, also originating from the East. Initially, mincemeat pies did contain meat, as it was a way of preserving meat. Today's recipes might contain beef suet, but most have eliminated meat altogether. I tasted mincemeat pie once (made with venison) and despised it, and Grandmama's sentiments about the concoction mirror my own.

Stir-up Sunday was the Sunday before Christmas when the Christmas pudding was made. The pudding originally contained meat, but that tradition has long since been replaced by the meatless version we know today. The pudding must be stirred in a clockwise direction to bring good luck all year. Historically, mincemeat was made the same day as Christmas pudding, and the tradition of stirring clockwise also applied to the mince. A final note about the holiday goodies served at Hefferwickshire House; for those who don't know, marchpane is marzipan. I chose to use the outdated term in favor of historical accuracy.

I needed a traditional Christmas carol in ¾ signature for the Christmas waltz in the story. After doing a bit of research I discovered *The First Noel* has Cornish origins and dates back to the Medieval period. Though the song wasn't published until 1823 in Gilbert's *Some Ancient Christmas Carols*, the popular carol was sung for centuries before that.

Because it's been an area of concern in some of my previous books, I'd like to address another important point. Occasionally, readers outside the United States become upset that I use American spellings or terms in my books set in Regency England.

Multiple factors influence an author's decisions about which spellings to use for their books. I chose American spelling simply because most of my reading audience is American, and my books are published in America. Were I to use British spelling, I can assure you, I'd receive emails and reviews criticizing that spelling. While I stick to a few British rules, such as *I shall* and *I shan't*, instead of I will and won't, I haven't extensively adopted other British grammatical rules and spelling.

I am confident that my readers in all areas of the world can adapt to slightly different spellings and word usages. After all, it's the romantic story that matters, right?

To stay abreast of the releases of the other books in the CHRONICLES OF THE WESTBROOK BRIDES, or my other upcoming releases, subscribe to my newsletter (the link is below) or visit my author world at collettecameron.com. Also, subscribers to my newsletter will have the opportunity to access a

Chronicles of the Westbrook Brides Reading Record.

I hope you enjoyed a romantic holiday escape to Regency England with the Westbrooks. If you liked this novella, please consider leaving a review. Reviews, even a few lines, really do help authors. Until next time…

Hugs,

Collette

Connect with Collette!

Join her Facebook Reader Group:

www.facebook.com/groups/CollettesCheris/

BookBub: bookbub.com/authors/collette-cameron

Facebook: facebook.com/collettecameronauthor

Instagram: instagram.com/collettecameronauthor/

Goodreads: goodreads.com/author/Collette_Cameron

WESTBROOK FAMILY

Gerhard Westbrook, 5th Duke of Latham (Deceased)
married to
Elizabeth (Libby) Everson, Dowager Duchess of Latham

Haygarth, Westbrook 6th Duke of Latham married to Margaret Ellison, Duchess of Latham	Edwin	Prentis	Maynard	Connell	Reuban (Mary-Wife)
Children: Adolphus Lucious Leonidas Darius Cassius Althelia Layton (Adopted Son) Fletcher (Adopted Son)	Children: Torrian Edina Asher Drake Chase Kade	Children: Rebecca Abraham Samuel Mathew Bethany Hannah Adam Caleb	Children: Fern Hunter Forest Skyler Luke Slater Cordelia	Children: Cole Kirk Bruce Reed Rowena	Children: Emerson Rogan Eva Laine Clarke Mynna

Gerhard's brother: Benedict Westbrook 2nd son (Wife Janet)				Gerhard's brother: Solomon Westbrook 3rd son (Wife Eliza)			
Charles	Henry	George	Fredrick	Joseph	David	Jane	Robert
Gerhard II	Mariam	George Jr	Simon	Cortland	Lawrence	Mary	Lucy
Caroline	Elizabeth	Martha	Doreen	Oscar	Terrance	Joanne	Ralph
Haygarth II	Judith	Mable	Dorothy		Margo	Sarah	Fulton
		Emma	Timothy		Bessie		Jude
		Priscilla			Hugh		Jonah
					Deborah		

Made in the USA
Las Vegas, NV
14 December 2022